Dear _____

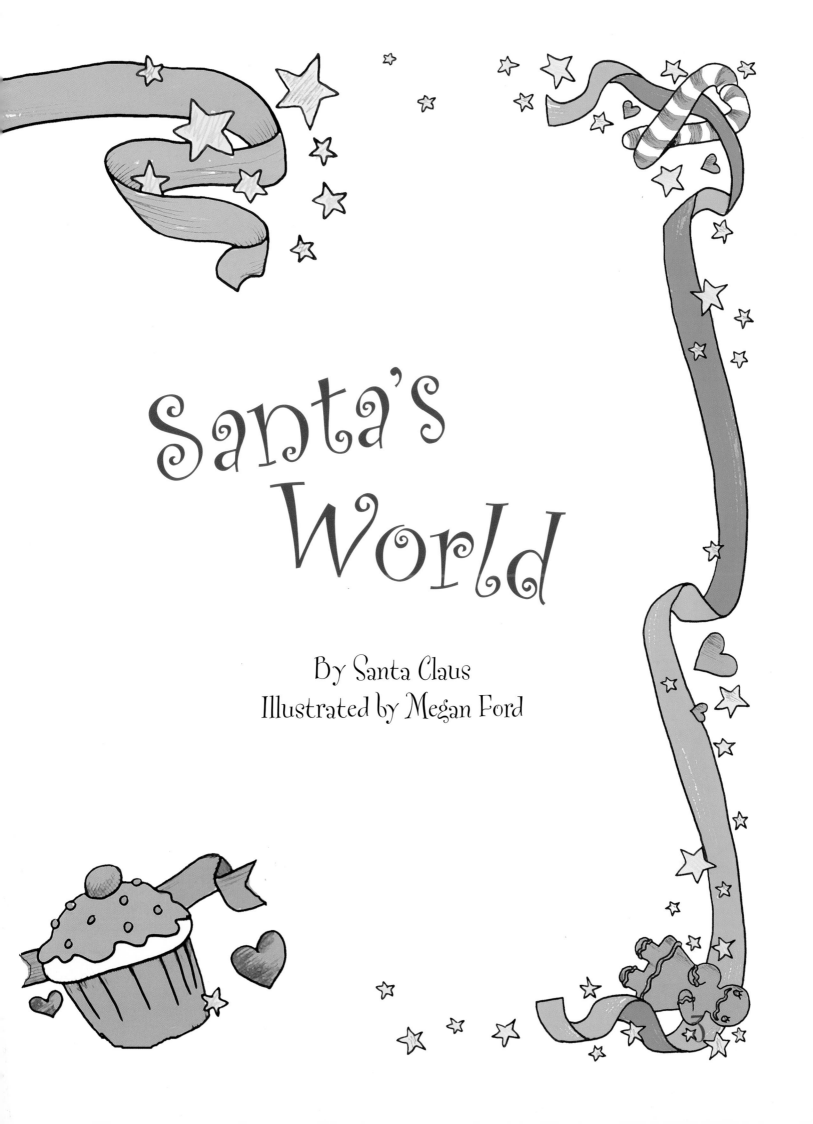

Santa's World

By Santa Claus
Illustrated by Megan Ford

Santa's World

Copyright © 2006 by Joe Moore

Illustrations by Megan Ford

Book design by: Carolyn LaPorte
Sound Engineer: Jonathan Richard Coe

Published by:
Kringle Enterprises
PO Box 394
San Clemente, CA 92674-0394
www.santasbooks.com

ISBN: 978-0-9787129-0-7
Library of Congress Catologing Number: 20069-06878

Printed in China
109876543

First Printing October, 2006

4

My life has been a series of miracles that have all come from two beings. The first is God who has made me Santa Claus in everyway physically and mentally. The other is my beautiful and incredible wife, Mary. In every aspect and in every setback, triumph, joy, sorrow, disappointment and of course, every happiness, these two have shared it with me and made every moment more special because of their presence in my life.

To say my life would be very different or incomplete without these two, is like saying an ocean would be a desert without water. My God loves me and all those that I love, so does my Mary. It is because of their miracle, that I can affect others. When you read this book from me, make sure you give thanks to them as well.

I certainly do.

Though many don't quite know the facts
It's really plain to see
Without my elves there wouldn't be
Many gifts under your tree.

The elves
they found
me working hard
So many years ago,

They invited me right there and then Up to their land of snow.

They showed me many marvels

And the tons of toys they store

All looking for a special home

Maybe one exactly like yours.

They built the houses and the shops

To service all these needs

They stored up lots of food and sweets

And even reindeer feed.

We all are living many years

Why it's impossible to tell

How long we've been

on this old earth

We hide our age so well.

Every elf becomes a specialist
And their craft they really know

Each toy is perfectly wonderful and

In each the quality shows.

13

And every elf's
important to me
Each one does lend a hand.
With the many varied tasks they do
Throughout this
Northern land.

14

There's Carrow, Christel, Jaime and more,
The elves are by the score.
Throughout each corner of the pole
They come through
every door.

And every one is precious to me

On their efforts I rely

Without them no one would ever see

A single reindeer fly!

They're smarter
than a good many folk

And always are so quick

As soon as something special I need

It arrives in just a lick

19

I think because they've lived so long

They've gotten all their smarts

Whether making toys, or wrapping gifts

Or even baking tarts!

But certain ones I really need

Or I couldn't do my best

These special elves all run the show

And I put them

to the test.

21

They have the most important jobs

They've worked hard to succeed

Much like my trusted reindeer

On my words they all pay heed.

"Now kids are all relying on us,"
I'll patiently explain

Christmas Eve's a special night
The meaning is so plain.

When God did give a special gift

And showed us all His love.

He gave to us His only Son

Said angels from above.

So on this night we recreate

For all who truly see

By giving gifts

and sharing love

And place them

by the tree.

The gifts we leave could not compare
For they are rather small
When compared to that
most mighty gift,
To that greatest gift of all.

But nonetheless
we'll do our part
And try to bring great smiles.
As Santa and his reindeer team
Cross many worlds
and miles.

So make sure that you go to bed

And are really fast asleep.

So I can leave our gift to you

And my promise

I can keep.

Then once again you'll wake to find
That I have been there too

And on this special

Christmas morn

You'll find our

gift for you.

32

Make sure you do say "Thank you"

But not to us alone

But to the Lord that's up above

It's His love that's been shown.

Have a
Wonderful
Christmas